A Gift For:

_____

From:

_____

All the way home, she
stared out the window.

The sun lowered closer to the horizon.

Later, at home, Marisol watched day turn into night.

That night, Marisol settled
into a deep dream.

She drifted through a sky swirling with colors.
The colors mixed, making too many to count.

In the morning, Marisol stood
waiting for the bus in the rain.
The sky was not blue.
She smiled.

At school, Marisol raced to the library.
She grabbed a dish and began adding colors.
This one, that one. She swirled the brush
to make an altogether new color.

Marisol then began painting on the wall.
A boy asked, "What color is THAT?"
"That?" Marisol said. "THAT is sky color."

Dedicated to Aldo Servino,
who took the blue paint away
from me and helped me paint—
and think—in sky color

Copyright © 2012 by Peter H. Reynolds

First edition 2012

Library of Congress Cataloging-in-Publication Data is available.
Library of Congress Catalog Card Number pending
ISBN 978-0-7636-2345-6

12 13 14 15 16 17 SCP 10 9 8 7 6 5 4 3 2 1

Printed in Humen, Dongguan, China

This book was hand-lettered by Peter H. Reynolds.
The illustrations were done in pen, ink, watercolor, gouache, and tea.

Candlewick Press
99 Dover Street
Somerville, Massachusetts 02144

visit us at www.candlewick.com

MARGRET & H.A.REY'S
Curious George
Visits a Toy Store

Illustrated in the style of H. A. Rey by Martha Weston

Hallmark
GIFT BOOKS

Houghton Mifflin Company
Boston 2002

This edition published in 2011 by Hallmark Books, a division of Hallmark Cards, Inc., Kansas City, MO 64141

Visit us on the Web at Hallmark.com.

The text of this book is set in 17-pt. Adobe Garamond.
The illustrations are watercolor and charcoal pencil, reproduced in full color.

ISBN: 978-1-59530-349-3
BOK1163

Printed and bound in China
APR12

This is George.

He was a good little monkey and always very curious.

Today was the opening of a brand-new toy store. George
and the man with the yellow hat did not want to be late.

When they arrived, the line to go inside wound all the way
around the corner. When a line is this long, it's not easy for a

little monkey to be patient. George sneaked through the crowd.
All he wanted was a peek inside.

George got to the door just as the owner opened it.
"This is no place for a monkey," she said.

But George was so excited he was already inside!
Balls, dolls, bicycles, and games filled the shelves.

There were so many toys —

George didn't even know
how some of them worked.

8

And how about these hoops?
What did they do?

George was curious. He climbed
up to pull one out of the pile.

It would not move.

George pulled harder.

Still it wouldn't move.

George pulled with all fours.

Suddenly there was a terrible crash.

Red, blue, green, and yellow hoops bounced up and down and everywhere.

"Look!" exclaimed a boy, bouncing up and down himself.

"Why, I haven't seen one of these in years!" said the boy's grandmother.

She put a hoop around her waist and gave it a spin.
George tried the hula hoop, too!

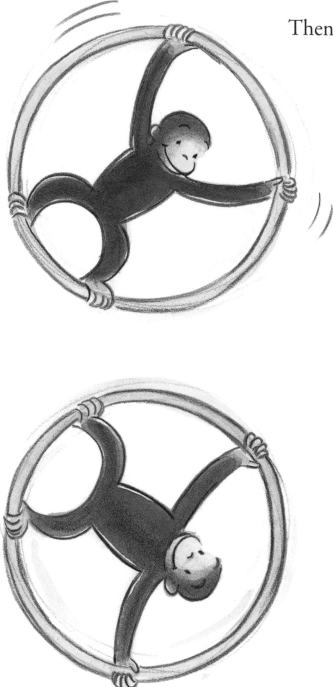

Then George pretended to be a wheel.

He rolled and rolled and....

13

Oops! He rolled right into the owner.

The owner shook her head. "I knew you were trouble," she said. "Now you've made a mess of my new store."

Again she tried to stop George.

And again George was too quick.

In only a second he was around the corner and on the highest shelf.

Below him, George saw a
little girl point to a toy out of
reach. "Mommy, can we get that dinosaur?" she asked.

George picked up the dinosaur
and lowered it to the girl.

She was delighted. So was the
small boy next to her.

"Could you get that ball for me,
please?" he asked George.

George reached up, grabbed the
ball, and bounced it to the boy.

"May I have that puppet way over there?" asked another girl.

How lucky that George was a monkey! He swung off the shelf, hung on to a light, picked up the puppet, and put it right into her hands.

"What a show!" shouted a boy.
The children held up their new toys
and cheered. What a commotion!

Immediately the owner came running,
and then came the man with the yellow hat.
"I think we've had enough
monkey business for one day,"
the owner frowned.

Just then a girl got in the long line to pay. "What a great store," she said. "What a great idea to have a little monkey helping you," her father told the owner.

"I guess you're right," the owner replied, and smiled.
Then she gave George a special surprise.

"Thank you, George," she said. "My grand
opening is a success because of you. Perhaps
monkey business is the best business after all."

The end.

Did you enjoy this book?
Hallmark would love
to hear from you.

Please send your comments to:
Hallmark Book Feedback
P.O. Box 419034
Mail Drop 215
Kansas City, MO 64141

Or e-mail us at:
booknotes@hallmark.com